This book belongs to:

Este libro pertenece a:

_____

Date:

Fecha:

_____

To all of our grandchildren with love - Grama Nancy and Grampa Bob

Publisher's Cataloging-in-Publication
(Provided by Quality Books, Inc.)

Sweetland, Nancy, 1934-
     If I could / author, Nancy Sweetland ; illustrator,
Robert Sweetland. -- 1st ed.
     p. cm.
     In English and Spanish.
     SUMMARY: A young boy imagines what he might do or be
if only he could, as fantasy combines with the everyday
world in this adventurous flight of fancy. Sometimes
it's best to be just who you are.
   Audience: Ages 4-8.
   LCCN 2002100432
   ISBN 0-9701107-7-4

   1. Dreams--Juvenile fiction. 2. Wishes--Juvenile
fiction. 3. Self-esteem--Juvenile Fiction. [1. Dreams--
Fiction. 2. Wishes--Fiction. 3. Self-esteem--Fiction.
4. Stories in rhyme.]   I. Title.

PZ8.3.S9954If 2002   [E]
                        QBI02-701363

Spanish translation by Creative Marketing of Green Bay, LLC

first edition

IF I
COULD
SI YO PUDIERA

Written by
Escrito por
Nancy Sweetland

Illustrated by
Ilustrado por
Robert Sweetland

If I could fly like a bird, I would.

I'd hop like a toad, too, if I could...

Si pudiera volar como un pájaro, yo lo haría.

Si pudiera, también saltaría como un sapo…

4

I'd swish like a snake,
or a fish in the lake. That is,
if I could, I would.

Yo me arrastraría como una culebra
o nadaría como un pez en el agua.
Si yo pudiera, lo haría.

I'd be a river that flows to the sea,

   or a far-shining star in the sky.

I'd like to be powerful once in a while

   like a strong wind blowing by...

   and I would, if I could, I'd try.

Yo sería como un río que desemboca en el océano,

   o una estrella luminosa en el lejano firmamento.

De vez en cuando me gustaría ser poderoso,

   así como el soplar de un fuerte viento...

   Yo lo haría, si pudiera. Yo trataría.

It would sometimes be fun

to be more than one--

like a hive of busy bees...

Algunas veces sería divertido

como un enjambre de abejas...

11

or a hill full of ants,

or a garden of plants.

Oh, wouldn't it? Wouldn't it be?

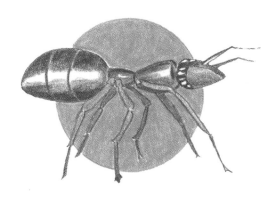

o un monte lleno de hormigas.

o un jardín de hermosas flores.

¡Oh! ¿No sería? ¿No sería?

13

I'd be a song that someone would sing,

or I'd be a bell that someone could ring...

or a cloud in the sky,

or a mountain so high--

if I could, I'd be everything!

Yo sería un canto que alguien cantaría,

o la campana que alguien tocaría...

o una nube en el cielo,

o una montaña muy alta--

Si yo pudiera, ¡sería todo eso!

14

15

I'd grow from a polliwog into a frog...

from a worm to a butterfly...

Me convertiría de renacuajo a rana...

de gusano a mariposa...

16

I'd live like a lizard under a log
and eat bugs, if I could. I'd try.

Yo viviría como una lagartija bajo un trozo de madera
yo comería insectos, si yo pudiera. Yo trataría.

19

I'd like to feel big as an elephant,

or small as the tiniest gnat--

Me gustaría ser grande como un elefante,

o muy pequeño como un mosquito--

or fat like a walrus,

or sleek like a seal,

or soft like a kitten-cat.

o gordo como una morsa,

o lisa como una foca,

o suave como un gatito.

23

I'd like to be able to spin a web

or live in a burrow deep...

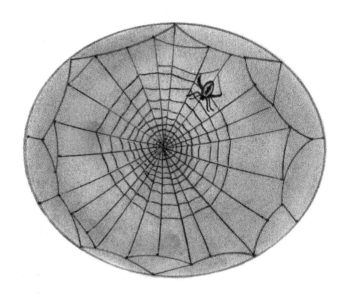

Me gustaría tejer una telaraña

o vivir en una conejera profunda...

I'd crawl on the ocean floor,

or nest on a mountain steep.

Me gustaría arrastrarme en lo profundo del océano,

o anidar en una montaña.

Oh, there's lots of things that I would be...

if I could. But I can't, and it's plain to see

that the world is just as it ought to be.

¡Oh! hay muchas cosas que me gustaría ser...

si yo pudiera. Pero no puedo, ¡claro!

el mundo es lo que es.

It's fun to think about all those things,

about flying and hopping and bells that ring...

but I know who I am, and that's who I'll be,

and I'm very glad that

I'm just me!

Es divertido pensar en todas esas cosas,

como volar, saltar, producir el sonido de las campanas...

pero sé quién soy, y eso es lo que seré,

y estoy muy feliz

¡De ser quién soy!

31

"If I Could" Glossary

English	Español
fly	volar
hop	saltaría
snake	culebra
wind	viento
sing	canto
big	grande
small	pequeño
mountain	montaña
world	mundo
fun	divertido